W9-ARX-716

Story play™

This book belongs to

_____.

This book was read by

_____

on

_____.

Are you ready to start reading the **StoryPlay** way?

Read the story on its own. Play the activities together
as you read!

Ready. Set. Smart!

THE THREE LITTLE PIGS

AND THE SOMEWHAT BAD WOLF

BY MARK TEAGUE

CARTWHEEL BOOKS · NEW YORK · AN IMPRINT OF SCHOLASTIC INC.

Copyright © 2013 by Mark Teague
Prompts and activities copyright © 2017 by Scholastic Inc.

All rights reserved. Published by Scholastic Inc., *Publishers since 1920.* SCHOLASTIC,
CARTWHEEL BOOKS, STORYPLAY, and associated logos are trademarks and/or registered
trademarks of Scholastic Inc.

Scholastic Inc., 557 Broadway
New York, NY 10012
Scholastic UK Ltd., Euston House, 24 Eversholt Street
London NW1 1DB

No part of this publication may be reproduced, stored in a retrieval system, or transmitted
in any form or by any means, electronic, mechanical, photocopying, recording, or otherwise,
without written permission of the publisher. For information regarding permission, write to
Scholastic Inc., Attention: Permissions Department, 557 Broadway, New York, NY 10012.

Library of Congress Cataloging-in-Publication Data available

ISBN 978-1-338-15774-1   10 9 8 7 6 5 4 3 2 1   17 18 19 20 21

Printed in Panyu, China   137
This edition first printing, June 2017
Book design by Doan Buu

ONCE THERE WERE THREE LITTLE PIGS.

They lived on a farm, as most pigs do, and were happy, as most pigs are. Then one day the farmer told them that he and his wife were moving to Florida. He paid the pigs for their good work and sent them on their way.

What good work do you think the pigs did for the farmer?

"Let's buy potato chips," said the first pig.
"Let's buy sody-pop," said the second pig.
"Let's buy building supplies," said the third
pig, who was altogether un-pig-like.

Reluctantly, the others agreed. The first
pig decided to build a straw house. Since
straw is cheap, he had plenty of money
left over for potato chips.

The second pig decided to build a stick house. Sticks are practically free, so he had lots of money left over for sody-pop.

How many bottles still have sody-pop in them? How many are empty?

The third pig decided to build a brick house.
Bricks and mortar are expensive, but the man
at the hardware store gave her a sandwich.

Soon the straw house was finished.
It was dusty and musty, but the first pig
did not mind. He rocked in his hammock
and ate potato chips.

Soon after that, the stick house was done. It was small and there was no room for a bathtub. But the second pig did not mind. He took a mud bath and drank sody-pop.

Brick by brick, the third pig worked on her house. Sometimes the other pigs would come by to watch. They had a wonderful time.

How would you describe each pig?

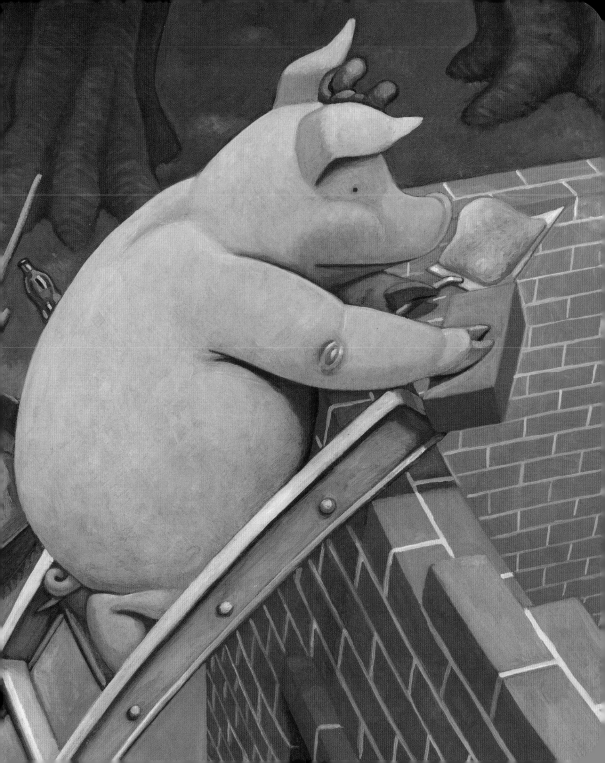

Finally, the brick house was finished. It was big, beautiful, and strong. The third pig was very happy. She filled a basket with vegetables from her garden.

Which house took the longest to build? Is that the house you would want to live in? Why or why not?

The next day a wolf came to town. He was very hungry and somewhat bad.

He went to a donut shop, but it was closed.

He went to a hot dog stand, but it was locked.

Finally, he went to a pizza parlor, but he wasn't allowed in. He left in a VERY bad mood!

Soon he came to a straw house. It smelled like pig.

"I like pig," he said, not in a friendly way. He banged
on the door.

"Who is it?" called the first pig.

"The wolf. Open up, or I'll blow your house down!"

"I think the door is stuck," said the pig.

So the wolf HUFFED . . . And he PUFFED . . .

AND HE BLEW THE HOUSE DOWN!

"I can't believe that worked!" he said. He had never blown down a house before.

Quickly, the first pig got on his scooter and sped away.

The wolf moved on, hungry but confident. He came
to another house, this one built of sticks.

"Same piggy smell," he said. He knocked on the door.

"Who is it?" called the second pig.

"Wolf. Open up, or I'll blow your house down! Trust
me," he added, "I've done it before."

"I think the door is jammed," said the pig.

So the wolf took an enormous breath . . .

And he HUFFED . . . And he PUFFED . . .

AND HE BLEW THE HOUSE DOWN!

"I'm amazed that works," he said.
Meanwhile, pig number two got on his
bike and rode away. The wolf was still
hungry — VERY, VERY hungry.

The hungry wolf came to a beautiful brick house. He noticed a familiar scooter and bicycle, and the house reeked of pig. The somewhat bad wolf rang the doorbell.

"Who is it?" called the pigs.

"The WOLF! Open up, or I will blow this house down!"

"Oh, no," said the pigs. "Not now, we are watching our favorite show."

The starving wolf took a HUMONGOUS breath. And he HUFFED . . . And he PUFFED . . .

And he HUFF-HUFF-PUFFED AND PUFF-HUFF-HUFFED AND HUFFY-HUFFY-PUFF-HUFFED.

After the huffing and puffing stopped, the third pig said, "Do you think he is still out there?"

The three pigs looked through the window and saw the wolf collapsed on the lawn.

"Look at the poor guy," said the first pig. "He's exhausted. Maybe he needs some potato chips."

The second pig added, "And some sody-pop."

The three pigs revived the wolf with some smelling salts and invited him in. The somewhat bad wolf was embarrassed. "I was so hungry I could not think straight."

"Have a potato chip," said the first pig.

"Have a sody-pop," said the second pig.

"Never mind that stuff," said the third pig. "Dinner is almost ready."

Since their houses were wrecked, the first two pigs moved in with the third pig.

"My house, my rules," she said. She made them clean their rooms before they went out to play.

The wolf stayed, too. But there was no more huffing and no more puffing. And he was hardly ever bad again.

Story time fun never ends with these creative activities!

★ Write Your Own Ending! ★

In this story of the three little pigs, the wolf and the pigs become friends! If you were writing your own story of the three pigs, what would your ending be? Would the pigs banish the wolf forever? Would the wolf win? Make up your very own ending, and ask an adult to help you write it down. Start your ending from the scene when the wolf comes to the brick house. Happy storytelling!

★ Hungry Habits ★

The three little pigs and the wolf all behave differently when they are hungry. One pig spends his money on chips, one on sody-pop—and the third pig waits and ends up with a free sandwich. When the wolf can't find food, he blows houses down! Finish these sentences about your own hungry habits.

When I'm hungry, I sometimes act . . .

My favorite food is . . .

I feel healthy and strong when I eat . . .